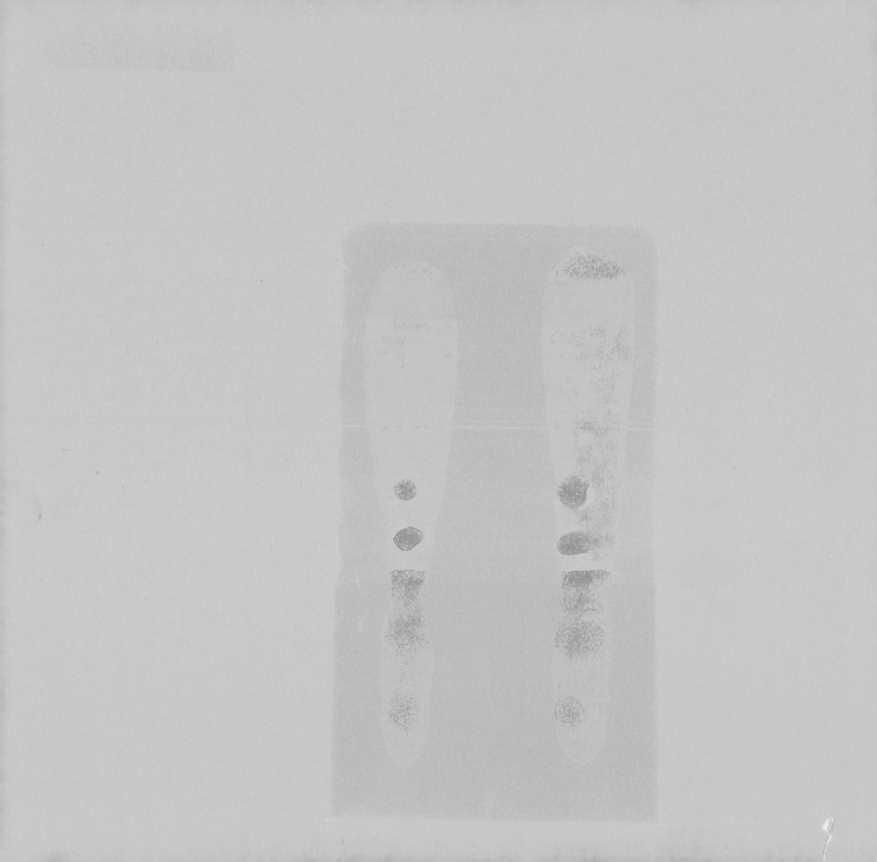

LITTLE RABBIT'S BABY BROTHER

CREATED BY LUCY BATE
STORY BY FRAN MANUSHKIN
PICTURES BY DIANE DE GROAT

Crown Publishers, Inc., New York

Library of Congress Cataloging-in-Publication Data
Manushkin, Fran. Little Rabbit's baby brother. Summary: Little Rabbit finds her own way of coming to terms with her new baby brother. [1. Babies—Fiction.   2. Brothers and sisters—Fiction.   3. Rabbits—Fiction] I. De Groat, Diane, ill.   II. Title.
PZ7.M3195Li   1986 [E] 86-2335
ISBN 0-517-56251-0

10 9 8 7 6 5 4 3 2

For Sam Jacobson Levin

One bright autumn day Father Rabbit asked,
"Who's in the mood for a picnic?"

"A picnic with cupcakes?" asked Little Rabbit.

"Yes, of course," said Mother Rabbit.
So off they went to the woods.

Mother and Father walked carefully because
Mother was expecting a baby.

"Watch what I can do!" Little Rabbit called.
She hopped in the clover, wiggling her ears.

"That's amazing," said Mother.

"Incredible," said Father.

"I love to hop!" Little Rabbit laughed.

When they finished their cupcakes, Little
Rabbit said, "Now close your eyes for a big
surprise."

"Flowers! How nice!" said Mother and Father.
And they wrapped Little Rabbit in a hug. "We
love your surprises!" Mother Rabbit smiled.
"And the new baby will love them too."

That night Mother began making a list. "We must buy plenty of bottles for the baby."

"Yes," said Father. "And don't forget blankets. We don't want Baby to catch cold."

"And booties," said Mother. "Lots of booties."

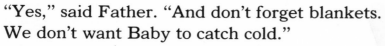

"Look, Mommy! Daddy!" Little Rabbit shouted. "I have a spaghetti mustache."

But Mother and Father didn't notice her. They were too busy thinking about the baby.

Little Rabbit started thinking too.

At bedtime, Little Rabbit sighed. "Mommy, our house is very small. Are you sure there's room for a baby?"

"I'm very sure," Mother Rabbit replied. "The baby needs just a little room."

A little room, thought Little Rabbit, drifting into a dream. *That baby's going to take MY little room and MY little bed, and I'll have to go away!*

In her dream, Little Rabbit put on her warm robe and went searching for a home.

"Come share our iceberg," called a polar bear family. But their hugs were very icy!

"Brrrrr." Little Rabbit woke up—fast! "Mommy!" she gasped. "Where's that baby going to sleep?"

"In a tiny little basket, in here." Mother smiled.

"That's a very good place!" Little Rabbit agreed. She snuggled back to sleep again, waving good-bye to the bears.

The next day Mother and Father made the baby's basket.

"I have a surprise!" Little Rabbit shouted. And she added a shiny red ribbon.

"Now we are ready for the baby," said Mother.

A few days later Baby Rabbit was born.

"Hi!" Little Rabbit smiled at him.

"*Waaaa*," cried Baby Rabbit.
"*Waaaa, waaaaa!*"

"Isn't he cute?" crooned Mother, holding the baby.

Little Rabbit held her ears.

"That baby's very noisy!" Little Rabbit groaned. "Maybe he should live outside."

"Who would take care of him?" Mother wondered.

"Birds would!" Little Rabbit giggled. "They'd feed him wiggly worms."

"Carrots taste much better," Father Rabbit said. "Let's all have some for lunch."

After lunch Father made hot chocolate.

"Here, little baby," Little Rabbit cooed. "You can have a taste of mine."

"Stop!" shouted Mother. "You'll hurt the baby!"

Little Rabbit scowled and sat down alone, watching her marshmallow melt.

"Drink up! It's delicious!" Father Rabbit urged.

Little Rabbit took a little sip. *"Umm,"* she said. "It's warm and sweet. I feel so good, I'm going to hop!"

"Ssssh!" whispered Father. "You'll wake the baby."

"I can't even hop in my house anymore!"
Little Rabbit cried—and hopped out the door!

"I'm hopping around the world," Little Rabbit yelled. The sun went down, but she kept right on hopping. Soon Little Rabbit was shivering.

Father shook his head and sighed. "I miss Little Rabbit so much."

Mother sadly hugged Little Rabbit's warm robe. "Yes, I miss Little Rabbit too."

"Close your eyes," called Little Rabbit, "for a big surprise."

Then she took one last HUGE hop—into her mother's arms.

Mother Rabbit smiled. "That was some big hop!"

"I'm getting big." Little Rabbit laughed.
"Well, of course," agreed Father. "You *are* a big sister."

"I'm a big sister," said Little Rabbit. It sounded really nice.

Suddenly Little Rabbit had a big idea.
Quickly, she drew a picture of herself hopping
and put it on her pocket. "This is my
Big Sister Robe," she said. "When I wear it, I
can help you with the baby."

"That's a splendid idea," Father Rabbit
agreed. "But your robe should have some
medals."

"Medals?" asked Little Rabbit.

"Yes indeed." Father smiled. "Big sisters
deserve lots of medals."

Mother snipped stars from Little Rabbit's old
booties. "These medals are for being such a
wonderful baby."

Father sewed on bells from Little Rabbit's first snowsuit.

"You earned these for making the best snow angels."

"Medals are fun!" Little Rabbit grinned. "And there's lots of room for more."

Little Rabbit wore her robe all through supper.
After dessert Baby Rabbit cried,
"Waaaaaaaaaa!"

"Poor little baby," said Little Rabbit. "I'll sing
you a lullaby:
La, la, la,
little teeny baby,
When you're as big as me
you can drink hot chocolate."

"That's a lovely song." Mother Rabbit smiled.
And she played along on her flute.

"The baby stopped crying!" Little Rabbit
whispered. She felt very proud.

"Would you like to hold him?" Father Rabbit asked.

"I think I would," Little Rabbit answered. She jingled her medals and wiggled her ears. Baby Rabbit smiled!

"Nice little baby," Little Rabbit cooed, and she smiled right back at him.

Then they all snuggled together on the soft old sofa as the baby fell asleep.

Late that night, the first snow fell.

Everyone in the family was fast asleep, and everyone was dreaming. Mother and Father dreamed of their children bringing flowers.

Baby Rabbit dreamed of
jingling and singing.

But Little Rabbit had the best dream of all:
She was holding her baby brother's hand
and hopping,
    and hopping,
        and hopping!